Love Songs of Narsinh Mehta

नरसिंह मेहता के शृंगार पद

Harsha V. Dehejia
Vijay Sharma

DK PRINTWORLD

Cataloging in Publication Data — DK

[Courtesy: D.K. Agencies (P) Ltd. <docinfo@dkagencies.com>]

Narasiṁha Mehetā, 1414-1481.

Love songs of Narsinh Mehta = Narasiṁha Mehatā ke Śṛṅgāra pada/Harsha V. Dehejia, Vijay Sharma.

pages cm

In Braj; translation in English and Hindi; study in English.

ISBN13: 9788124608036

1. Braj poetry. 2. Braj poetry — Translations into English. 3. Braj poetry — Translations into Hindi. I. Narasiṁha Mehetā, 1414-1481. Songs.Selections. Braj. II. Narasiṁha Mehetā, 1414-1481. Songs. Selections. English. III. Narasiṁha Mehetā, 1414-1481. Songs. Selections. Hindi. IV. Dehejia, Harsha V., translator. V. Sharma, Vijay, 1962-, translator. VI. Title. VII. Title: Narasiṁha Mehatā ke Śṛṅgāra pada.

DDC 891.4712 23

ISBN: 13: 978-81-246-0803-6

First published in India in 2015

Design: Paul Crupi, Ottawa, ON, Canada

Text: Harsha V. Dehejia

All images are from the Dehejia Collection of Krishna Art

Printed and published by:
D.K. Printworld (P) Ltd.
Regd. Office : 'Vedaśrī', F-395, Sudarshan Park
(Metro Station: Ramesh Nagar), New Delhi - 110 015
Phones : (011) 2545 3975; 2546 6019; Fax : (011) 2546 5926
e-mail : indology@dkprintworld.com
Web : www.dkprintworld.com

Acknowledgement

Selecting *shringara-bhashit padas* from the vast writing of Narsinh Mehta, translating them and then transforming them into paintings require the effort and support of many people.

The following are therefore gratefully acknowledged:

1. Shri Labhshankar Purohit who took the trouble of explaining the many nuances of Narsinh's writings to me. In his company I felt the closeness of a scholar and an elder.
2. Shri Jawhar Baxi for selecting the *shringara-bhashit padas* and then going over them, translating and explaining every word. He is a friend and I could turn to him with so many questions.
3. Prof. Neelima Shukla-Bhatt of Wesleyan College, Massachusetts, USA for her scholarly interpretation of Narsinh's work.
4. Prof. Sachin Kelkar of M.S. University, Vadodara, whose thesis on Narsinh was a valuable resource.
5. Shri Utkarsh Majumdar whose theatrical insights into Narsinh's *padas* were most helpful.
6. Padma Shri Vijay Sharma who was the master artist of the project. It was left to him to interpret the *padas* to the various artists and supervise the creation of paintings. Without his brilliant *kalam* and his keen sense of the aesthetics of miniature paintings this project would lack whatever colour and charm that it possesses.
7. Shri Nitin Sharma who diligently handled the Devanagari fonts.
8. Shri Susheel Mittal and Rajendra Agrawal of D.K. Printworld who treat authors like members of their family and who convert manuscripts into books and portfolios with professional care and efficiency.
9. Shri Ashit Desai, who not only lent his melodious voice to these songs but also helped us with the manuscript.

Sourcebook for Narsinh Mehta's *padas*.
Narsinh Mehta ni Kavya Kritiyo
Dr Shivlal Tulsidas Jaisalpura
Sahitya Samshodhan Prakhashan
Ahmedabad, 1981.

ARTISTS

1. Mewar, Savant Singh Naruka 2. Bikaner, Sanjeev Sharma
3. Kangra, Parikshit Sharma
4. Jain, Kailash Chand Sharma 5. Late Kangra, Mukesh Dhiman
6. Kishangarh, Mahendra Singh Sisodia
7. Chaurapanchashika, Devender Sharma 8. Basohli and Guler, Vijay Sharma
9. Popular Mughal, Girdhar Khinchi, 10. Kangra, Parikshit Sharma

Narsinh venerates Krishna, painting by Vijay Sharma

Variation on a Popular *Bhajan* by Narsinh Mehta

वैष्णव जन तो तेने कहिए, जे कृष्ण ना मधुर रूप ने स्मरे रे।
झेणे कान्हुड़ो नी वनमाला जोइ अने बांसुरी नी धुन शांभळी रे ।। १ ।।

वृंदावन नी कुंज गली मा झेणे कान्हुड़ो ने गोपियों संग रमतो जोयो रे ।
वाच काच मा अखिलम मधुरम, सबक जे वांसलड़ी थी अनुभवे रे ।। २ ।।

झेणे शरद नी रूड़ी राते, व्हालुड़नो गोपी साथे महारास जोयो रे ।
धन्य जेने प्रेम ना रंग थी वैष्णव जन नू मनड्डु रंगयू रे ।। ३ ।।

आद्य तू, मध्य तू, अन्तय तू, मारो सर्वस्य छे तू मारो श्री हरि ।
मदन नंदकुमार गोवर्धनधारी, मारो कान्हुड़ो छे श्री हरि ।। ४ ।।

कान्हा तुज मुज वच्चै अन्तर नथी, शृंगार मा नथी अद्वैत नू नेती नेती ।
कान्हुड़ो तू माया नी मिथ्या नथी, तू व्हालुड़ो छे सत्य हृदय भरी ।। ५ ।।

नानु सारखु गोकुळियू व्हाला ए वांसलड़ी नी धुन थी वैकुंठ किधु रे ।
कान्हुड़ो ए करयु मारू वृंदावन रूड्डु, वैकुंठ मारे नथी जवुं रे ।। ६ ।।

कुमकुम ना पगले अवो व्हाला कुमकुम ना सर्व मंगलमय करो रे ।
निहारू तन मन थी तनेज जहां जहां मने दीठू तारू माधुर्य रे ।। ७ ।।

Harsha V. Dehejia

Radha–Krishna, painting in Basohli style by Vijay Sharma

Narsinh Sings to Krishna

निहम वसामी वैकुंठे योगिनाम हृदय न
च मद भक्त यात्रा गायन्ती तत्र तिष्ठामी नारद
I dwell nor in Vaikuntha, nor in the hearts of *yogi*s
Where my devotees sing, there I am, Narada.
— *Padma Purana*

If there is one poet whose name is written in letters of gold and whose star shines the brightest in the firmament of Gujarati poetry it must be that of Narsinh Mehta (1408–65) and it is in the fitness of things that he is considered the *adi-kavi* of Gujarat. He is what Homer is to Greek and Valmiki is to Sanskrit. This is not to deny poets writing in Gujarati before Narsinh but none of them remains in the collective memory of Gujaratis. Premananda (1690–1780) and Dayaram (1833–1909) were worthy successors to Narsinh.

While Narsinh is widely recognized as a Vaishnava *bhakti* poet of medieval India, and an important persona of the Bhakti movement which started from the south and moved to the north and west of India, what is not so commonly known is that he is also a *shringara kavi*, a poet of romantic love. It is said that his *bhakti* has *prem* and his *prem* has *bhakti*, and so that his poetry is regarded as *shringara bhakti kavya*. Essentially *shringara* is the romantic celebration of the other, and when the other is none other than Krishna, *shringara kavya* becomes Krishna *bhakti*, as it is only Krishna who can be human and divine at the same time. *Bhakti* essentially implies knowing oneself through veneration of the other, and when the other is none other than Krishna, *shringara bhakti* becomes even more special.

The earliest known *shringara kavya*s are to be found in *Gathasaptasati* of Hala and the Sangam poetry of the Tamils, the latter perhaps pre-dating the former. It were the

Tamilian Alvars, and Andal in particular, who inaugurated the ecstatic and emotional *bhakti* of Krishna and wrote evocative poetry embracing both the longing and belonging of Krishna. However it was in the *dashama skanda* of the tenth-century *Bhagavata Purana* that *shringara bhakti* attains its Sanskritic legitimacy. Jayadeva in his *Gita-Govinda* moves away from the *bhakti* of the *Bhagavata*, and in introducing Radha makes *shringara* more human and turns way from the Advaita of the Bhagavata to Dvaita, a transformation that was to lead to Gaudiya Vaishnavism of Chaitanya and into Ritikavya.

Coming about 200 years after Jayadeva, Narsinh once again champions the Bhagavata and returns to *shringara bhakti* as he celebrates Krishna through amorous verses and divine surrender. Narsinh was aware that the purists of the world at large may not understand the true meaning of s*hringara bhakti* and misunderstand it as voyeuristic and therefore would not accept his *shringara bhakti* as true *bhakti*, for he wrote:

हे हरि लोक कहे नरसैंहो लपटी।

There are many miraculous episodes connected with his life but there is one that is worthy of being noted. Narsinh was brought before Raja Mandalik and accused of singing lewd songs. When Narsinh pleaded that in those songs also was his love of Krishna the king imprisoned him and only when the garland on the image of Krishna in the temple appeared on Narsinh in the morning that the king released him. This apocryphal account highlights how *shringara rasa kavya* (romantic songs) can be understood only by a *sahradaya* (a cultivated heart).

It was the beginning of the fourteenth century and Patan, the ancient capital of Gujarat, was ruled by Muslims. Fearing persecution, 68 Nagara families went to Saurashtra. One among them was Krishnaray Pandya, who had three sons: Jivenrai, Bansirai and Narsinhrai, who settled in Talaj. Narsinh, was born in 1408, grew up in modest surroundings and even when he a teenager, he was engaged to Manek from Junagadh. In 1427 Narsinh lost his mother and after this his sister-in-law took over the household and she would often taunt him. After one such insult Narsinh went to the Gopanath Temple and took refuge there for seven days and nights. Shiva was pleased with his penance and asked him for a boon. Narsinh it is said asked for a

vision of the Rasa-Lila in Vaikuntha. He was so awe struck by this vision that he forgot that he was holding a flare in his hand and even as he watched in ecstasy his hand was burnt. It was during this vision that he realized that in his love for Krishna he had ceased to be a man and he wrote:

पुरुष–पुरुषानन लीन थयु माहरुं
सखी रूपे थयोमध्य भाव।

The only man for Narsinh was Krishna and all of us who lovingly venerated Krishna were women at heart. This was the standard Vaishnava doctrine that Narsinh followed.

Narsinh moved to Junagadh, which was his wife's natal home and there he stayed in a temple singing the glory of his beloved Krishna. Narsinh was a non-sectarian Vaishnava and although he was a brahmin he agreed to sing in a Harijan colony for which he was ostracized. Narsinh's *bhakti* did not take him way from this world and he remained a *sansari* and not a *vairagi* for he fulfilled all his worldly duties and never abandoned his family. He died in the year 1465 at the age of 57.

Narsinh's *shringara bhakti* was an admixture of Vedanta and the Bhagavata. He was essentially a Vedantin and subscribed to its monistic view and when he sings:

जागी ने जोऊँ तो जगत दिसे नहि, उंधमा अटपटा भोग भासे।

and

अखिल ब्रह्मांडमां एक तुं श्री हरि, जुजवे रूपे अनंत भासे।

and

आद्य तुं मध्य तुं अंत्य तुं श्री हरि।

also there is a romantic togetherness with a hint of Advaita when he sings

तुज मुज वच्चे व्हाला अन्तर नथी।।

Narsinh shows the characteristic stamp of Advaita Vedanta in his songs, but unlike the Mayavada

of Shankara's Advaita Vedanta Narsinh was a dyed in the wool Vaishnava and took his stand on the *Bhagavata Purana* and in particular Krishna of the *dashama skanda*. He remained tied to the *sakara* Krishna, or the visual and audible form of Krishna and his *sakara svarupa* (His sensual form), never opting for the *nirguna* and *nirakara*. Having followed poets like Bilvamagal and Jayadeva and preceded both Vallabhacharya and Chaitanya, Narsinh was a non-secterian Vaishnava and celebrated the *shringarik* Krishna of the Bhagavata and he is sometimes referred to as a Bhagavata *kavi*. It is possible that both Nimbarka and Jayadeva influenced him although in different ways. Nimbarka was a Dvaitin and the Nimarka Sampradaya had a presence in medieval Gujarat and this may have tempered his Advaitic views so that he could embrace both the transcendence of Vedanta and the immanence of the Bhagavata, and sow the seeds of Shuddha Advaita of Vallabhacharya that was to come later. Without the Dvaita–Advaita of Narsinh there cannot be *shringara bhakti*, for it is the Dvaita that fosters sensual celebration of the other and it is the Advaita of Vedanta that brings in surrender to the transcendent. Narsinh's Vedanta was a coming together of Advaita and Dvaita, just as the human condition has both sleep and the waking state, with sleep being a metaphor of Advaita and the waking a paradigm of Dvaita.

Narsinh played a pivotal role in the Vaishnava *bhakti* movement that was sweeping all across the north and the west of India where devotion to a personal god, rather than to an abstract idea of the absolute was taking hold of the Hindu mind. Narsinh's *bhakti* however was coloured with the hues of romance, it was woven with the threads of *shringara*, it was fragrant with the aroma of amorous pleasures and was alive with the throb of song and dance. Vallabhacharya and the Maharashtrian *sant*s were devoted to specific temples, Vallabhacharya to Shrinathji Temple of Nathdwara and the *sant*s to Vithoba Temple at Pandharpur. Narsinh who preceded them remained a non-sectarian Vaishnava. His Krishna was in a temple of Junagadh where he sat and sang his songs.

Jayadeva's songs were a big influence on Narsinh and some of Narsinh's *pada*s have the same rhythm and texture as that of Jayadeva. It was Jayadeva who through his flawless Sanskrit created his *asthapadi*s which had both melody and rhythm and

Narsinh was able to carry this forward with his medieval Gujarati:

के रस जाणे ब्रजनी नारी, के जयदेवे पीधो रे
उगरतो रस ढलतो हतो, नरसैंये झोंटी ने लीधो रे

Even at a time when the written word was not that prevalent it is interesting how poets in different parts of the country were connected and influenced each other and one could speculate that the spoken word must have been carried by priests and pilgrims, and people of trade and commerce, as they crisscrossed the country on foot or bullock carts. This is what created the collective unconscious of the tradition. That Gujarati of Narsinh was an admixture of Braj and Sauraseni both of which were spoken in north-west India. Narsinh did not have an *ashrayadata* (patron) and he sang in the language of the people. His felicity with language and his choice of words was such that it had both *lalitya* (softness) and *gita* (melody). His *pada*s were disarmingly melodious and easy on the tongue so that they were sung in homes and *haveli*s, in chowks and around *chabutara*s, by *rasika*s on a moonlit night, by brides and housewives, as *prabhtiya*s as she wakes the household in the morning and *bhakta*s in the courtyard. He sang in the folk style and although he may have been familiar with *raga*s his *pada*s have a simple rhythm and lilting melody. Such was the beauty and charm of his words for were they not inspired by the honeyed notes of Krishna's flute? The first line of his *pada*s, which very often is the refrain, makes a dramatic opening statement and the narrative that follows builds on this powerful opening line.

His songs were addressed directly to Krishna, it was as if Krishna was sitting in front of him and he would address him with intimate and endearing words like *vahludo*, *vahlaji*, *kanhudo*, *goyaliya*, *rasiyo*, *shamaliyo*, *nandji na lad*, *pranjivan*, *mithda*, and *bhola nath*. Only someone whose love is sincere and sacred can take such liberties with Krishna.

With his honeyed words Narsinh was able to create a whole universe of romantic feelings and recreate the idyllic Vrindavana in our mind's eye, but that Vrindavana with the footfalls of Krishna becomes a Vaikuntha for Narsinh:

न्हानुं सरखुं गोकळियुं
म्हारा व्हाला ए वैकुंठ कीधुं रे।

so that even the heavenly Vaikuntha is not interesting

म्हारुं वृंदावन छे रुंडु रे, वैकुंठ नहि आवुं रे
व्रज नी नारी विठ्ठल काजे सर्व तजीने चाली रे।
भणे नरसैंयो ए तो मोहन संग म्हाली रे।
कुमकुमने पगले पधारो, राजा कुमकुमने पगले।
राति मोल धारो म्हारा व्हाला राति ऋतुं रुडी रे।
राति दांते हसे राधाजी केमान चुडी रे।।

Narsinh's song of a *nayika* who abandons her worldly duties reminds one of the *abhisarika*s, notice

व्रज नी नारी विठ्ठल काजे सर्व तजीने चली रे।
भणे नरसैंयो अे तो मोहनसगें म्हाली रे।

When clouds gather and Ghanashyam's presence is felt both in the sky and on the earth where he dances, words such as *rumjhum* bring in the sweet sound of tinkling bells and words like *mehulo gaje ne madhav nache* suggest thunder and lightning and the whisper of Raga Megh Malhar fills the air.

He invites Krishna with words of colour, especially red

कुमकुमने पगले पधारो, राजा कुमकुमने पगले।

for the suggestion here is that Krishna's presence is *mangalmaya* like *kumkum.*

also

राती मोल धरो म्हारा व्हाला, राती रुतु रुडी रे।
राते दन्ते हसे राधाजी, कायेमान चुड़ी रे।

Cherish red love, for the beautiful season
is tinged with red!
Rosy is the glow on laughing Radha's teeth
And scarlet are the bangles on her exquisite hands.
Cherish red, love, for the beautiful season
is tinged with red!

Narsinh's world is the idyllic Vrindavana where there is forever spring, where every tree is a *kalpavriksha,* where *gopi*s play amorously with Krishna under the *kadamba* tree and the flute of Krishna animates the parrot and the peacock, the *lata* and the *vriksha*, and Vasanta has painted the world red and there is joyous abandon everywhere. He writes:

आ ऋतु रुडी रे, म्हारा व्हाला, रुडो मास वसंत।
रुडा ते वन मा केसु फुल्या, रुडो राधाजीनो कंठ।
अती रुडु वृंदावन शोभतु, रुडु ते जमना तीर।
अती रुडी गवालनी मंडली, रुडो ते हलधर वीर।
रुडुं रंगे रबाब बाजे, तरुनी ले करताल चतुर नारी
चंग वजदे, मोरली मदनगोपाल।
रुडा रंग कुमकुम केसर ना, रुडा मुख तम्बोल।
अति रुडो नरसौंयांनो स्वामी, नित नित झाकम झोळ।

Keeping with Vaishnava doctrine, Narsinh approaches Krishna with *stree bhava* (a woman's heart), for after all Krishna is the only male and a woman's love for her beloved is the purest. While maintaining the *stree bhava* Narsinh, from time to time, wishes to be a *duti/sakhi* (a messenger) and this may be a direct influence of Jayadeva.

And even more, Narsinh is so struck by the sensual beauty of Krishna that very often he sees the form of Mohini in Krishna equating the two in their beautiful form. He writes:

ब्रह्म अे नथी घडी भामिनी अे तो आपे बनीने आवीरे।
भण लोकनुं नेज तरुणी ऐ तो छबी छबीली बनावीरे।।

and

हरि आव्या छे नारीना वेशेरे अेने कोई जुवोरे।
शिव ब्रह्मा जेनु ध्यान धरेछे तेने जोई दुःखड़ा खुवोरे।।

Narsinh sings effortlessly of the beauty of a woman, her sensual charm, her coquettish gait, her coy demeanour, her romantic moods, her dalliance with her *sakhi*s and above all her loving togetherness with Krishna, that one begins to feel that one is hearing pure love songs. But it is towards the end of the *pada* that Narsinh's *shringara* turns into *shringara bhakti*, when he uses words like *bhane narsinhyo* (Narsinh's *swami*) that the sensuality of *pada*s turns into spirituality and our hands that were clapping and our feet that were thumping to the music and the rhythm of the *pada*s as we participated in the *lila*s of Krishna are transformed into the serene silence of reverence and veneration of Krishna, as we are transfixed and spellbound at the majesty and grandeur of Krishna. It is as if we, who were taking part in the Rasa-Lila, are led by Narsinh into a vision of the divine Krishna.

We do see some frankly erotic songs in Narsinh's oeuvre. Notice:

In my garden the mango tree has blossomed
and mangoes ripe are dripping with nectar
wake up and relish them, my slender lord
I will pluck them for you to enjoy.

The image of the mango tree is oft recurring theme in Narsinh's songs and can be read both as a harbinger of spring as well as expressing lust.

also

Do not untie the strings of my *choli*
the fruit of my breasts is not good enough for you.

Narsinh's *shringara* is generally devoid of *vipralambha* or *viraha*. The heart-wrenching longing that one sees in Kalidasa or the sixteenth-seventeenth-century Ritikavya is missing in Narsinh. However one notices the passion of longing in *pada*s like

Cold cold is my bed in winter
but for my love who will embrace me passionately?

also

Don't wake me up vigorously
You will break my delicate waist.

Narsinh in his lifetime did not commit his songs to writing for he was not a court singer nor did he have a noble patron; all he w ould do would be to sit in the temple and sing for and to Krishna. It did not matter whether anyone was listening to him, for his songs were meant for his Krishna for it was for Him that he sang. The only extant documents that are available from Narsinh's time are Jaina sacred texts like *Kalpasutra* and also Gujarati poetry. Jaina poetry has an admixture of old Gujarati and Ardhamagadhi and this makes its language very terse. These Jaina poetry while remaining theologically important could not reach the popular Gujarati imagination. Narsinh on the other hand laid the foundation of the Gujarati literary tradition, fired the popular imagination and remains an indelible part of the memory of Gujaratis. Narsinh's songs in being both oral and dramatic, and which have in them the simultaneous existence of the romantic and the erotic, the metaphysical and the ethical, have an abiding place in the hearts and minds of the Gujaratis and are alive even today.

The earliest written record of Narsinh's songs dates to CE 1612, which raises the question whether they are a true and faithful reproduction of what he actually sang in his lifetime or whether the language could have changed in the 200 years that had elapsed. It would be safe to assume that in a couple of centuries that had elapsed the old Gujarati that he had used had changed into the medieval Gujarati that we see in his *pada*s today. Some however are of the opinion that the language of the *pada*s that are available today are not different from what Narsinh actually sang.

Notwithstanding that debate one can say that Narsinh expressed his *shringara bhakti* with soft and mellifluous words, his *pada*s were *shabdasiddha* (expressed through beautiful words) as well as *layasiddha* (lyrical), it had in them *shabdalamkara* rather than *arthalamkara*, for it was his love for Krishna that adorned his words and it is Krishna's presence that makes the words *krishnamaya*, for were not the words sung for Krishna himself? Those words were both sonorous and well sculpted, *netrendriya* and *karnendriya*, visual as well as aural, for they created evocative visual images and mellifluous sounds rather than literary meanings and were driven by more by their sound and not so much through semantics. Narsinh's poetry was sung, his *pada*s were songs, they were performed and not just read, they had to be realized and enjoyed and not contemplated and thus it is that its sound was as important as its meaning.

Narsinh was a Nagara Vaishnava but strict religious rites and rituals did not matter to him, for to opt for them and sacrifice *shringara bhakti* would be, as wrote, to equate stones with jewels. Through his soulful songs he connected directly

with Krishna, he spoke to Him and He in turn participated in his songs, it was as if his beloved Krishna was sitting in front of him listening to him. Notice:

मे गायो भ्रम ते परम आनंद शुं,
कर्मना जीव ते मरम बोले।
धर्म धुरंधर तुजने जाणे नहि,
रत्न गुंज करे एक तोले।।

Narsinh's songs are coloured by the hues of his mind, they throb with the rhythm of his heart, there is in them the glow of love and the radiance of *bhakti* and even today as we sing or listen to them, they lift us and bring us face-to-face with Krishna, such is their strength and veracity. It is as if Narsinh, through his songs, exhorts us to abandon our banal chores and like the *gopi*s rush to be with Krishna, for in his songs is the very presence of Vrindavana. For Narsinh's Krishna is not a distant god in the temple, we do not have to perform any rites or rituals to venerate him, He does not ask for fasts or penance, but all He wants is for us to participate with Him in his *lila*s and *krida*s and be touched by His mellifluous love. Narsinh's songs recreate the magic and the charm of Vrindavana, it is as if in his songs we listen to the rustling of the *kadamba* leaves, the chirping of the birds, the dance of the peacock and the whisper of the Jamuna. Narsinh is quintessentially a poet of the Bhagavata.

Like a true *bhakta* Narsinh's concept of *mukti* was not release from the cycle of birth and death but instead to be born again and again so that he could celebrate and serve Krishna, notice:

हरिना जन तो मुक्ति ना जांचे,
जांचे जन्मोजनम अवतार रे।
नित्त्य सेवा नित्त्य किर्तन ओच्छाई,
निरखवा नंदकुमार रे।।

and

निरखने गगनमा कोण घुमी रहयो, तेजहुं तेजहुं शब्द बोले।
श्यामना चरणमा इच्छु छुं मरण रे अहिन्य कोई नथी कृष्ण तोले।।

The minutae of philosophic arguments and matters of logic and reason did not interest him for all he wanted was to indulge in his love of Krishna, luxuriate in His sensual form, be touched by His mellifluous love and venerate Him with his songs of love and be born again and again to celebrate His love for Krishna.

प्रेम रस पाने तुं मोरना पिच्छधर
तत्त्वनुं टुपणु तुच्छ लागे

O One! bedecked with peacock feathers
serve me the draught of love's ambrosia
logic and reason are arid.

And then again

Vain are all your efforts and like unseasonal rain
you have wasted your human birth.

The Vedantic *neti-neti* was not for Narsinh, for that would imply negation of the beautiful world of the sounds and sights of Krishna, instead it was *iti-iti*, indulgence and affirmation of every aspect of Krishna's sensuality for only through that he could become *krishnamaya*.

इन्द्र ब्रह्मा जेने लेष अनुभवे नहिं
नेति नेति करी निगम भाखे।
तेह महाराज तमो मुझने कृपा करो
दासने चरण पासे राखो।।

Narsinh's life mission was to celebrate and venerate Krishna through *shringara bhakti*, to make his words *krishnamaya*, and ensure that his songs resonated with the sounds of *krishnaprem*. When the sounds of *shringara bhakti* are followed by the hushed silence of *shringara rasasvadana* perhaps we reach the primal sounds of Narsinh's songs:

अचेत चेतन थयुं
अवतणो अघा गायो
सुनि उठी मारि आद्य वाणी

Narsinh's legacy is timeless, his imprint on the Gujarati mind is deep, he lives in the collective memory of Gujarat, the whisper of *Vaishnava jana to* bring to mind Gandhiji, his influence on poets through the centuries is significant and it would be hard to find a Gujarati poet who has not been touched by Narsinh. In particular one sees his resonance in poets like Rajendra Shukla, Dayaram and Nanhalal.

To realize and be animated by the love of Krishna were to open the floodgates of *ananda*, and once Narsinh, and we, along with him, experience that *ananda* from the *shringara rasa* of Krishna, can *brahmananda* be far behind?

प्रीत नी रीत तो परम वल्लभ सदा हेत न जीव तो हेते रूठे।
जन्मो जन्म लीला रास गावता लहण ना वहण ते द्वार छूटे।।

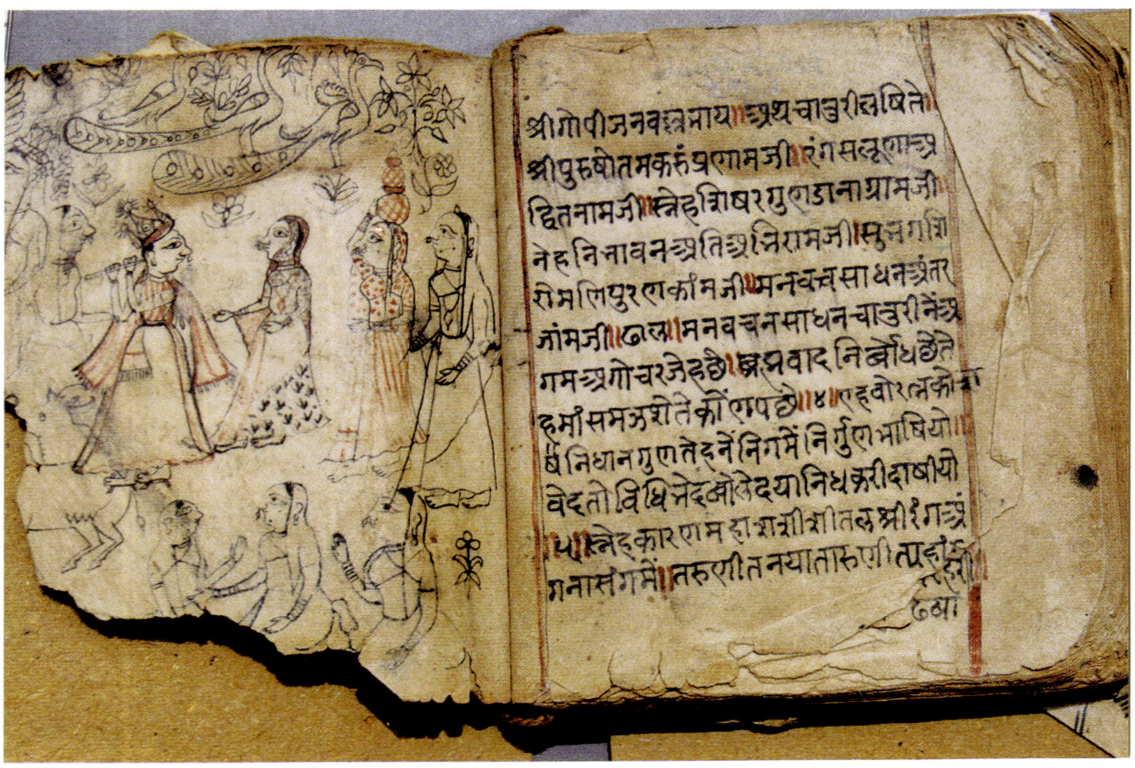

c. 1742

Fluting Krishna, Kota, eighteenth century

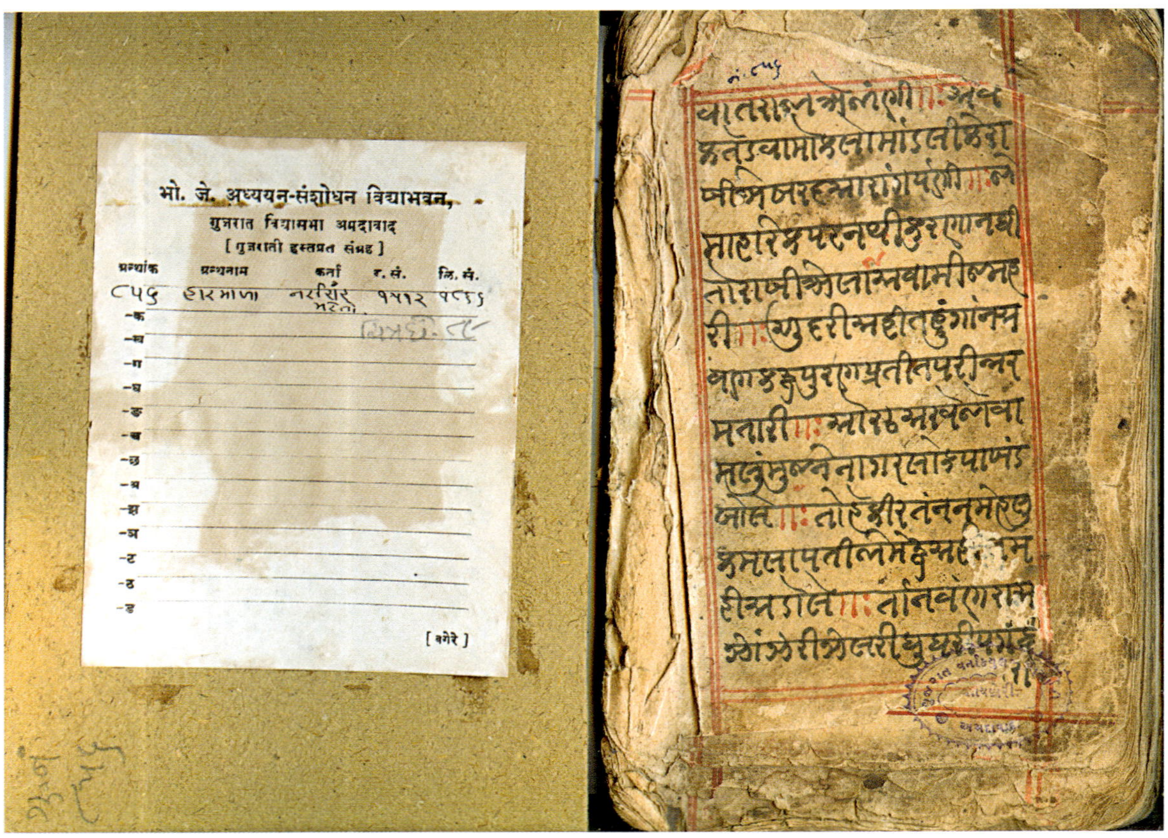
भो. जे. अध्ययन-संशोधन विद्याभवन,
गुजरात विद्यासभा अमदावाद
[गुजराती हस्तप्रत संग्रह]
ग्रन्थांक ग्रन्थनाम कर्ता र. सं. लि. सं.
[वगेरे]

Manuscript pages of Narsinh Mehta's poems from the B.J. Institute, Ahmedabad

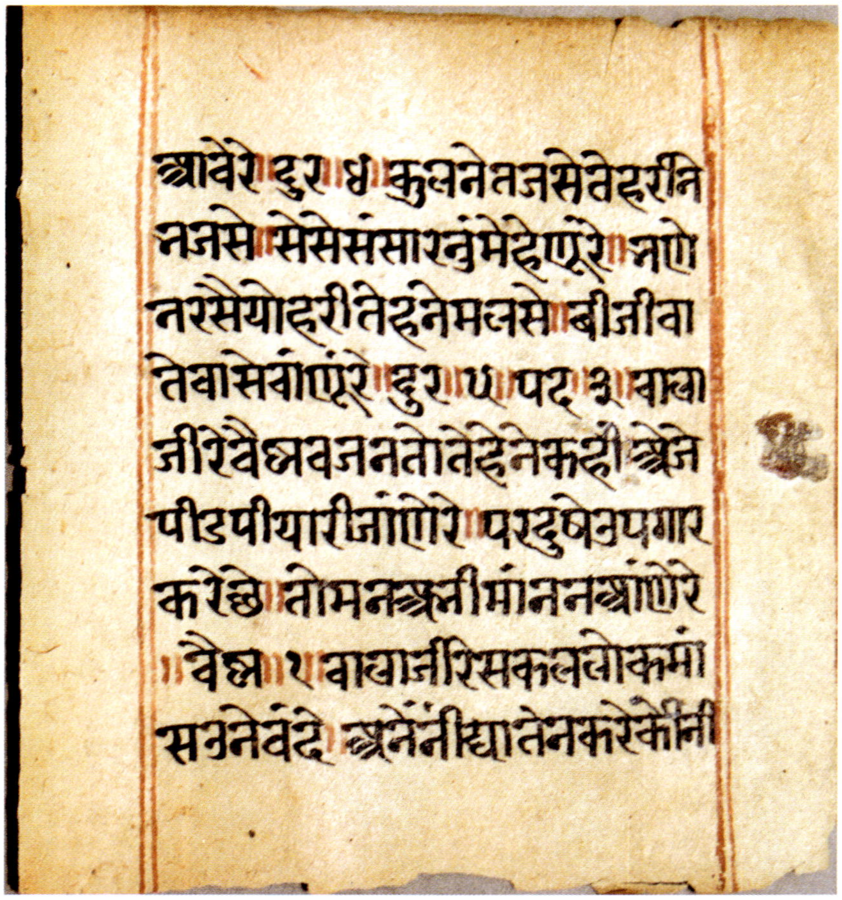

Undated

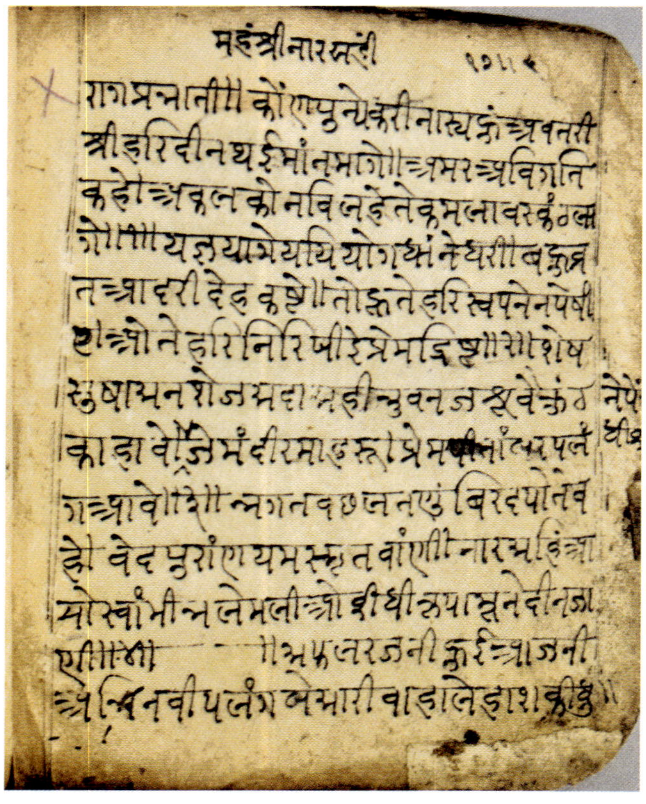

c. 1611

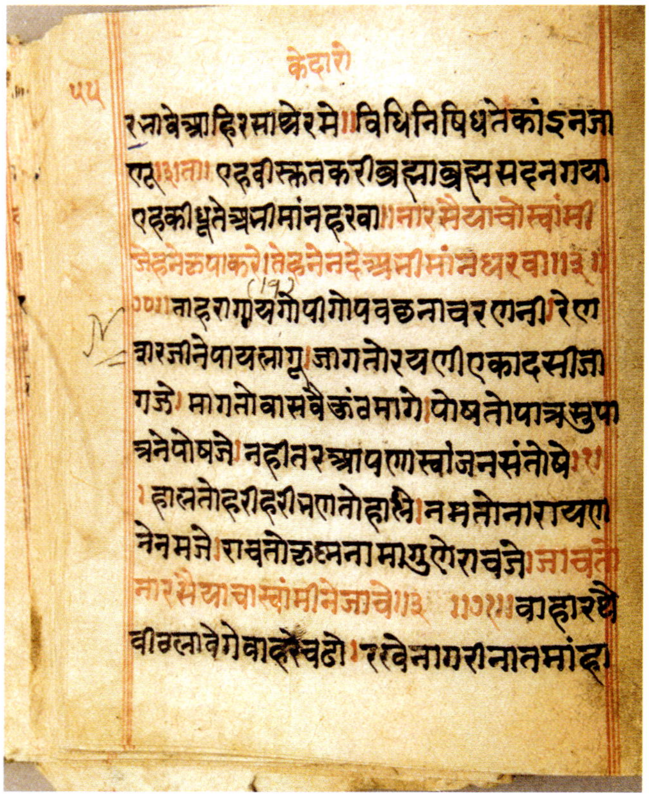

c. 1701

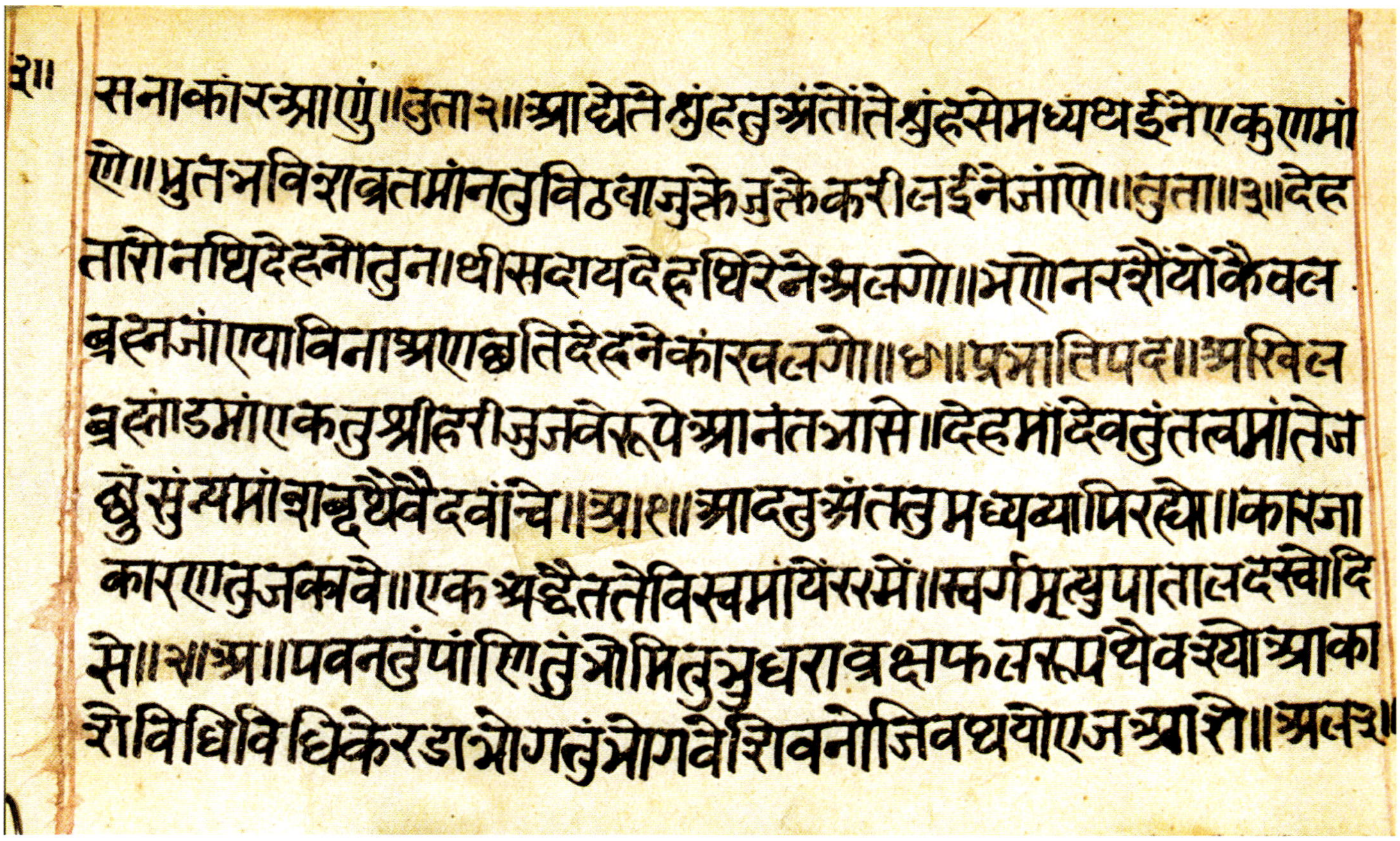

Undated

Manuscript pages of Narsinh Mehta's poems from the B.J. Institute, Ahmedabad.
Photograph: Neelima Shukla-Bhatt

9

आजनो मांडवडो मारो मोगरडे छायो
राधाजीने संगे व्हालो रमवाने आव्यो।
गोफणिये घुघरड़ी धमके रेशमनि दोरी
शामळियो शामळो रंगे राधिका गोरी।
दूध दही ने करमलडो मांहे साकर धोळी
म्हारा वहालाजी आरोगे पीरसे भ्रमर भोली।
सोळेते शणगार सज्या सरखि ओढन साड़ी
श्रीवृंदावनमां विट्ठल साथे रमत मांडी।
अखंड अहेवातण मारे ए वर रूडो
नरसैयांचा स्वामीए मुजने पहेराव्यो चूड़ो।।

Today the pavilion of love is full of jasmine flowers
and Krishna enters it with Radha for romantic pleasures
as bells on the hair ornament
strung with silken threads resound
dark is Krishna and fair is Radha.
She serves sweet milk and curds and Krishna relishes
beautified with the sixteen adornments
and draped in fine clothes
she plays amorously with Krishna, she is the eternal bride
says Narsinh that Krishna has
adorned my arm with bangles.

आज प्रेम का मण्डप मोगरे के फूलों से सजा हुआ है। कामकेलि हेतु कृष्ण ने राधा के साथ मंडप में प्रवेश किया। वेणी में रेशमी धागों से बंधे नन्हें घुंघरू मधुर ध्वनि कर रहे हैं। कृष्ण श्याम वर्ण हैं और राधिका गौर वर्ण। राधा ने कृष्ण को मीठे दूध और दही से प्रसन्न किया। सुंदर वस्त्रों और सोलह श्रृंगार से सजी राधा ने कृष्ण के साथ रतिक्रीड़ा की। दोनों शाश्वत प्रेम में रत हैं। नरसी कहते हैं कि कृष्ण ने मेरी बाँह को कंकण से विभूषित किया है।

Artist Savant Singh Naruka

Style Mewar

२

भोळी रे भरवाडण हरिने वेचवा चाली
सोळ सहस्त्र गोपीनो व्हालो मटुकीमा घाली
अनाथना नाथने वेचे आहीरनी नारी
शेरीअे शेरीअे साद पाडे ल्यो कोई मुरारि
मटुकी उतारी मांहे मोरली वागी
व्रजनारी ने मुख जोता मूरछा लागी
ब्रह्मांदिक इंद्रादिक सरखा कौतक अे पेखे
चौद लोकना नाथने कांई मटुकीमा देखे
गोवालणीनां भाग्ये प्रगटया अंतरजामी
दासलडांने लाड लडावे नरसैंनो स्वामी

Innocent milkmaid went to sell Hari
Beloved of 16,000 *gopi*s she has put Him in a *matuki*
This *ahir* woman is trying to sell Hari
the lord of the orphans and helpless
From street to street she shouts please buy Hari
She put down her *matuki*
and from that she heard the flute.
In that she saw the face of Krishna and she fainted
and all the gods of heaven and earth came
to see this wonder of seeing Hari the lord
of fourteen worlds in a *matuki*.
It was the good fortune of this milkmaid
that thus she saw the indwelling lord in her pot
Krishna cherishes the milkmaids.

सोलह हज़ार गोपियों के प्रिय हरि को मटकी में डालकर कोई भोली–भाली गोपी बेचने को निकली है। दीन अनाथ का पालन करने वाले हरि को वह गोपी बेचने की कोशिश कर रही है। वह गलियों में घूम–घूमकर पुकार रही है "कृपया कृष्ण ले लो"। उसने जब अपनी मटकी रखी तो उसमें से बांसुरी की ध्वनि सुनाई दी। तब उसे मटकी में कृष्ण की छवि दिखाई दी और वह अचेत हो गई। धरती और आकाश के सभी देवता इस चमत्कार को देखने के लिए आए कि चौदह भुवनों के स्वामी मटकी में विराजमान हैं। अवश्य यह इस गोपी का अहोभाग्य है कि उसे अपनी मटकी में अन्तर्यामी कृष्ण के दर्शन हुए। कृष्ण गोपियों से इस भाँति लाड़ करते हैं।

Artist Sanjeev Sharma

Style Bikaner

३

चाल रमीअे, सही! मेल मथवुं मही
वसंत आव्यो, वनवेल फूली
म्होरिया अंब, कोकिला लवे कदंब
कुसुम कुसुम रह्या भ्रमर झूली
पहेर शणगार ने हार, गजगामिनी
क्यारनी कहुं छु जे चाल उठी
रसिक मुख चुंबीअे वळगीअे झुंबीअे
आज तो लाजनी दुहाई छुटी
हेते हरि वश करी लाहो ले उर धरी
कर ग्रही कृष्णजी प्रीते पळशे
नरसैयो रंगमा अंग उन्मत्त थयो
खोयेला दिवसनो खंग वळशे

O *gopi* let us go, let us play
abandon churning the curd
spring is here and all the creepers in the forest
have blossomed
mango blossoms are everywhere
the *kokila* sings on the *kadamba*
the wasps dance over the flowers.
Rise O *gajagamini*! Do not tarry
adorn yourself and let us go
let us kiss Krishna and embrace Him
this is not the time to be shy
fill your heart with love and He will hold your hand
Narsinh too (this spring becomes a *gopi*) and is
coloured with these feelings and he will make
the best of the lost time.

हे सखी, यह दही बिलोना छोड़ो और खेलने चल। बसंत आ गया है वन में लताएँ नए फूलों से लदी हुई हैं, हर ओर आम बौराए हुए हैं, कदम्ब पर कोयल कूक रही है, कमल–दल पर भ्रमर गुंजार कर रहे हैं। हे गजगामिनी! उठो। देर मत करो, अपना श्रृंगार करो और चलो। चलो हम कृष्ण का आलिंगन करें और उनका चुंबन लें, यह लजाने का समय नहीं है। अपने हृदय को प्रेम से भरो, कृष्ण तुम्हारा हाथ थामेंगे। नरसी भी इस रंग भरे भावों से ओत–प्रोत है, वह भी इस समय का सदुपयोग करेगा।

Artist Parikshit Sharma

Style Kangra

४

तट जमुनानुं अति रळियामणुं रे, जेणे तट खेले गोपी–गोवाळ
जीवन अमारो वचे वहालमो रे, व्हालो मारो वाये वेण रसाळ
तमो तरुवर अमो वेलडी रे, वहालो मारो विरहिणीयांची वेल
गुणवंता संगाथे अमारे गोठडी रे, जी रे रढियाळो रंगनी रेल
मुखडुं जोई जोई व्रजजन महालतां रे, हां जी अमो हिडंता
व्हालाजीने झळके कुंकुंम कांबळी रे, उपर भ्रमर करे गुंजार
व्हालाजीने सोहे (कुसुम) मोगरो रे, हरि मारा हैडा केरो हार
चोदिश चमके रे वनिता वीजीळिरे, वहालो मारो गांजे नंदकुमार
महाजलाधीशां रे श्याम श्यामा वदे रे, मुने गमे शामळियानो शोर
नरसैयाचा स्वामी प्रत्त्ये अमो लेणला रे, वहालो मारो पूरण जुगल किशोर

Beautiful indeed is the bank of Jamuna
and on its bank the *gopi*s and *gopa*s play
Our beloved Krishna is there too playing the melodious flute
He is the tree, the refuge of the creeper
she the woman who longs.
We play with him who is full of *guna*s, the fountainhead of bliss
and beautiful colours emerge from it.
Seeing this the people of Vraj dance around Him
red *kamli* covers Him and bees sing about Him
adorned with jasmine flowers, Hari is my heart's necklace
maidens from all four directions look
like lightning in the centre and Hari roars like thunder
Hari and Radha are like the waves of
the vast ocean and speak to each other
We enjoy the fullness of the young couple
The lord of Narsinh is the perfect Jugalkishore.

जमुना का तट निश्चित ही सुरम्य है जिसके तट पर गोप–गोपियाँ क्रीड़ा करते हैं। हमारे प्रिय कृष्ण भी वहाँ बंसी बजाते हैं। वे वृक्ष हैं तो हम विरहिणीयाँ लताएँ हैं। जब उस गुणों से भरे कृष्ण संग हम रमण करती हैं तो सुंदर रंग अवतरित होते हैं। यह देख वृजवासी उसके इर्द–गिर्द नृत्य करते हैं। वे लाल कमली से आवेष्टित हैं और उनके ऊपर भ्रमर गुंजार करते हैं। मोगरे की माला से सजे हरि मेरे हृदय के हार हैं। चारों दिशाओं से आई युवतियाँ विद्युन्माला की भाँति हैं जिनके मध्य कृष्ण गरजते हैं। कृष्ण और राधा विशाल सागर की लहरों की भाँति (परस्पर घुल–मिलकर) वार्तालाप कर रहे हैं। युवा युगल की पूर्णता का हम आनन्द ले रहे हैं।

Artist Kailash Chand Sharma

Style Jain

५

चालो सखी! वृंदावन जईअे, जहां गोविंद खेले होळी
नटवरवेष धर्यो नंदनंदन, मळी महावन टोळी
एक नाचे एक चंग वजाडे, छाटे केसर धोळी
एक अबीर–गुलाल उडाडे, एक गाय भांभर भोळी
एक एकने करे छमकला, हसी हसी ले कर ताळी
मांहेमांहे करे मरकलां, मध्य खेले वनमाळी
वसंत ऋतु वृंदावन प्रसरी, फूल्यो फागण मास
गोविंद–गोपी रमे रंगभर, जुअे नरसैयो दास

O *sakhi*! Let us go to Vrindavana
where Govinda plays Holi
Nandanandana is attired in dancer's clothes
and people have gathered in the enchanted forest
One dances, the other plays the drum
and yet another sprays saffron
someone sprays *abir* and *gulal* as one cow
is transfixed and moos
everyone plays in joyous abandon
clap and smile at each other
and Krishna in the middle plays Holi.
Vasanta is here and has spread all over Vrindavana
as the month of Fagun arrives
Govinda and *gopi* play with colours
as Narsinh watches spellbound.

हे सखी, चलो वृंदावन चलें जहाँ गोविंद होली खेल रहे हैं। नंदनंदन ने नर्तक की पोशाक पहन रखी है और लोग उस जादुई वन में एकत्र हुए हैं। कोई नृत्यरत है, कोई ढोलक बजा रहा है, कोई केसर तो कोई अबीर–गुलाल छिड़क रहा है। एक गऊ तो एकटक देख रही है। हर कोई आनंद से सराबोर है और एक–दूसरे को छू रहे हैं। बीच में कृष्ण होली खेल रहे हैं। सारे वृंदावन में वसंत का खुमार है क्योंकि फागुन मास फूल गया है। गोपी संग गोविंद की होली–लीला को नरसी आश्चर्य से देख रहे हैं।

Artist Mukesh Dhiman

Style Late Kangra

६

जागो रे जशोदाना जिवण ! व्हाणलां वायां
तमारे ओशीके मारां चीर चंपायां
पासुं मरडो तो व्हालां ! चीर लेऊ ताणी
सरखी समाणी साथ जावुं रे पाणी
पंखीडा बोले रे, व्हालां ! रात रहि थोडी
सेजलडीथी उठो, व्हालां ! आळसडी मोडी
साद पाडुं तो व्हालां ! लोकडियां जागे
अंगूठो मरडुं तो व्हालां ! पगना घूघरा वागे
जेने जेवो भाव होय, तेने तेवुं थाये
नरसैयाचो स्वामी विना, रखे व्हाणलुं वाये

Awake Yashoda's life, dawn is here
under your pillow are my clothes
just turn and I will pull away my *odhani*
and go with my *sakhi*s to fetch water
the birds are singing my beloved
and the night is about to end.
Get up from your bed give up your indolence
if I wake you up with my voice
then the neighbours will hear
if I twist your toe your anklets will sound
one becomes what one thinks
unless Narsinh's Lord wakes up the day will not begin.

यशोदा के प्राण उठो, भोर हो गई है। आपके तकिये के नीचे मेरे वस्त्र हैं। थोड़ा सा सरको तो मैं वस्त्र ले लूं और अपनी सखी संग जल भरने जाऊँ। हे प्रिय! रात्रि समाप्त हो गई है और पक्षी चहचहा रहे हैं। अब आलस्य त्यागो और बिस्तर छोड़ो। मैं अगर बोलकर जगाऊँगी तो सभी पड़ोसी सुनेंगे। मैंने अगर पाँव के अँगूठे से हिलाया तो नूपुर बज उठेंगे। तुम्हारे भाव ही जीवन को रूप देते हैं। जब तक नरसी के स्वामी जाग नहीं जाते, तब तक जीवन हो ही नहीं सकता, कोई जीवन नहीं।

Artist Mahendra Singh Sisodia

Style Kishangarh

૭

क्षितिरस तरुशाखाओ प्रसर्यो, मनसिज नयणे वसियो रे
रुदेभाव कुचमंडळ पूर्यो, आव्यो रतिपति रसियो रे
अतलिबळ वनस्पतिनाथे उलटपालट कीधुं रे
अखिल ब्रह्मांडनु अमृत लेई, जुवतीने वदने दीधुं रे
अद्‌भुत बळ आप्युं अबळाने, नर कायर वर अंगे रे
हसवुं वनवेलीनुं आप्यु, कोकिला–स्वर मुख–रंगे रे
योग–वियोग विमुखने आप्यो, भोग भक्त–भगवान
तप–तपस्या कर्मजडने आप्यां, नरसैयाने गुणगान

The sap of the earth spreads through
the trees and Kama resides in our eyes
love comes to reside in the breast and
the consort of Rati has arrived
Krishna, the lord of trees, has created chaos
He gave the nectar of the entire cosmos to the face of the
young maidens and empowered them
gave them the laughter of the creeper
and painted their throat with the voice of the *kokila*
union and separation he gave to the faithless
pleasure to the devotee, penance and rites to the pious
and to Narsinh he gave the joy of singing his glory.

धरती की सोंधी सुगंध वृक्षों में फैल रही है। काम हमारे नेत्रों पर विराजमान हो गया है। पयोधरों पर आसीन है रति का प्रिय मदन। वृक्षों के अधिष्ठाता कृष्ण ने हलचल मचा दी है। उसने ब्रह्माण्ड का अमृत सभी युवतियों के मुख पर उंडेलकर उन्हें शक्तिशाली बना दिया है। उन्हें लताओं की भाँति हँसी दी है और कोयल की कूक से उनके कंठ चित्रित किए हैं। मिलन और विरह नास्तिकों को दिए हैं, भक्तों को सुख और नरसी को उसकी महिमा गाने का आनन्द दिया है।

Artist Devender Sharma

Style Chaurapanchashika

ट

गोरी! तारे त्राजुडे रे मोह्या मोह्या मुनिवरराया रे
रूप स्वरुप कळयु नव जाये, कोई दीसे छे ईश्वरी माया रे
रूमझुम रूमझुम नेपुर वाजे, गोफणे घुंघरी धमके रे
शीश दामणी अेणी पेर सोहे, जेम गगन वीजळी चमके रे
निलवट आड करी केसरनी, मांहे मृगमदनी टीली रे
आंखलडी जाणे पांखलडी हींडे लीलाअे लाडगहेली रे
आ कंचवो तमे क्यां सिवडाव्यो! शणगट वाळयोशुं धारी रे!
आ वेणी तमे क्यां रे गूंथावी, जेणे मोही छे व्रजनी नारी रे!
चंचल दृष्टे चोदिश निहाळे, मांहे मदननो चाळो रे
नरसैयाचो स्वामी जोवा सरखो, कोई अे सुंदरीनुं वदन निहाळो रे

Sages and rishis are infatuated with your body marks
your beauty is beyond our comprehension
all we see in it is the maya of God.
Your ankle bells sing and throb, the bells tinkle in your hair ornament
your head ornament sparkles like lightning in the sky
your forehead sports the saffron mark
and the tilak of musk
your eyes are like petals, your gait is coquettish
where did you have your *choli* stitched?
And who taught you how to cover your head?
and who did your braid?
The maidens of Braj are infatuated
and they look in all directions with restless eyes
as if to spread the message of Madan
Look at the beautiful maiden for
in her is the presence of Krishna(Mohini).

आपके शरीर पर बने छाप तिलक पर सारे ऋषि–मुनि मंत्रमुग्ध हैं। आपका सौंदर्य हमारे आकलन से परे है। हम सब इसमें ईश्वर की माया देखते हैं। आपके पग–नूपुर ध्वनि से गुनगुनाते हैं, वेणी के आभूषण में भी नन्हें घुंघरू झंकृत होते हैं। आपके सिर का आभूषण ऐसे चमकता है मानो आकाश में विद्युन्नमाला। आपका ललाट केसर और कस्तूरी के तिलक से सुशोभित है, मानो बसंत की मधुर ऋतु आ गई है। वन में केसू के फूल खिल उठे हैं और राधा की वाणी में मधुरता आ गई है। यमुना का सुरम्य तट और सारा वृन्दावन सुन्दरता से भर उठा है, जो मदन का संदेश प्रकट कर रहे हैं। इस अनिन्द्य सुंदरी (मोहिनी) को देखिए, जिसमें कृष्ण का प्राकट्य है।

Artist Vijay Sharma

Style Basohli and Guler

६

मेहुलो गाजे ने माधव नाचे, रुमझूम वाजे पाये घूघरडी रे
ताल–पखाज वजाडे गोपी, व्हाली वजाडे वेणुवांसलडी रे
दादुर–मोर बपैया बोले, मधुरी शी बोले कोयलडी रे
पहेरण चीर, चरणांने चोळी, ओढण आछी लोबरडी रे
धन्य जमुनातट, धन्य बंसीवट, धन्य धन्य आ अवतार रे
धन्य नरसैयानी जीभलडी जेणे गायो राग मल्हार रे

As the clouds thunder Madhava dances
and his anklets resound ever so sweetly
the *gopi*s sound the drums as Krishna plays on the flute.
Frogs, peacock and birds sing
and even the *kokila* sings a sweet song.
Surrounded by men and women
dressed in traditional attire, *pehran*
and *choli* and *chania*.
Blessed is the bank of Jamuna where the flute is heard, blessed is this *avatara*
blessed is the speech of Narsinh
who sings Raga Malhar.

ज्यों ही मेघ गरजते हैं, माधव नृत्य करने लगते हैं, उनके नूपुर मधुर ध्वनि करते हैं। गोपियाँ कृष्ण द्वारा बंसी बजाते ही ढोल पर थाप देने लगती हैं। दादुर, मोर, पपीहा गाते हैं और कोयल मधुरता से कूकती है। पुरुष और स्त्रियों ने पेहरान, धोती, चोली और चनिया पहन रखा है। धन्य है जमुना का किनारा जहाँ मुरली की धुन गूँजती है। कृष्ण का यह अवतार भी धन्य है। नरसी का कथन भी धन्य है, जो राग मल्हार में गा रहा है।

Artist Girdhar Khinchi

Style Popular Mughal

१०

मने रोके छे कानवर दाणी रे, नहि जाऊं जमना पाणी रे
अेकवार जमना पाणी रे गयातां व्हाला, मारी साथे सैयर समाणी रे
वृंदावनने मारग जातां, मारी नवरंग चुंदडी ताणी रे
जोरे पाणी मोकलवांरे होय तो, साथे मोकलो सैयर समाणी रे
मरकलड़े मारां मन हरी लीधां, हुं तो लालचमा लपटाणी रे
नरसैंयाचा स्वामीनी संगे रमता, हुं तो मोहन संगमा माणी रे

I will not go to the river to fetch water
as Krishna accosts me there.
Once I had gone to the Jamuna
to bring water along with my friends
when on the way to Vrindavana he pulled my *odhani*.
If you want me to go to the river
please send my friends with me
as he has stolen my greedy mind
and now I start playing with Narsinh's *swami*.

मैं नदी से जल भरने नहीं जाऊँगी, क्योंकि वहाँ कृष्ण मुझे परेशान करते हैं। एक बार मैं सखियों के साथ जमुना से पानी लाने गई थी तो वृंदावन की राह में उसने मेरी ओढ़नी खींच ली थी। यदि मुझे पानी भरने के लिए भेजना है तो मेरी सखियों को भी साथ भेजें। क्योंकि उसने मेरा चंचल मन चुरा लिया है और मुझ में लालच आ गया है। अब मैं नरसी के स्वामी के साथ खेलने लगी हूँ।

Artist Parikshit Sharma

Style Guler

Vaishnava *mahant* in a shrine, Kangra, 1820-30